I0780320

COPYRIGHTS

ACKNOWLEDGEMENT

Thank you, Michelle Marcus, for your unwavering support and dedication to creating a book that resonates with our youth. Your encouragement and enthusiasm have been a wonderful support.

Thank you, Carol Killman Rosenberg, for your exceptional editing expertise and for your invaluable assistance in shaping this book. Your keen eye and insightful suggestions have been instrumental in bringing this project to life.

Thank you Chip Evra for the wonderful photos of Shelley and Pip.

Thank you Brent Eite for your friendship and beautiful drone photos.

Thank you Gina Holt with Wild About Birds Inc for your friendship, support and wisdom.

Thank you to the Ark Wildlife Rescue! Thank you for taking Pip and helping regain his strength. The work you do for our wildlife is a gift.

Thank you to my social media friends who encouraged me to share Pip's tale children's book. You are a wonderful community and very important part of this book.

DEDICATION

This book is dedicated to Pip the Pelican. Thank you for sharing your journey and friendship.

You continue to give hope to people of all ages by inspiring us to trust, persevere and love.

Pip's Fishy Adventure

A TRUE STORY

WRITTEN BY

SHELLEY LYNCH, PHD
WITH MICHELLE MARCUS

PHOTOGRAPHS BY
SHELLEY LYNCH

It was lunchtime on the Indian River in Florida and a young pelican swooped and dove for fish in the blue waters of New Smyrna Beach.

He hovered above the shimmering water, watching a dolphin named Momma Jade and her baby, Opal cuddle and hunt for fish.

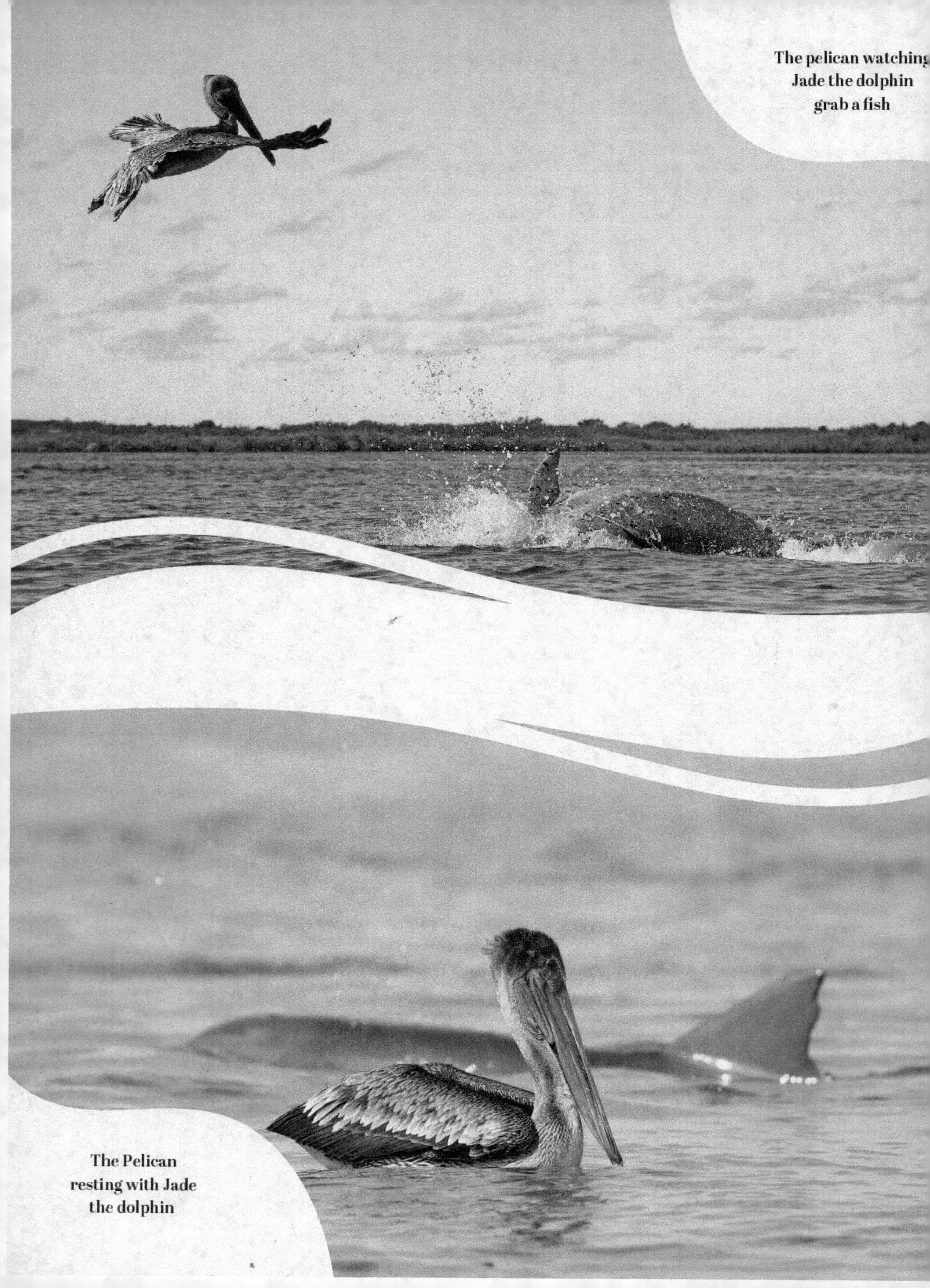

The pelican watching
Jade the dolphin
grab a fish

The Pelican
resting with Jade
the dolphin

From above, the pelican spotted Mikey the great egret fishing in the shallow waters, while Spot, a smaller egret, seemed to dance with his wings spread wide as he chased fish.

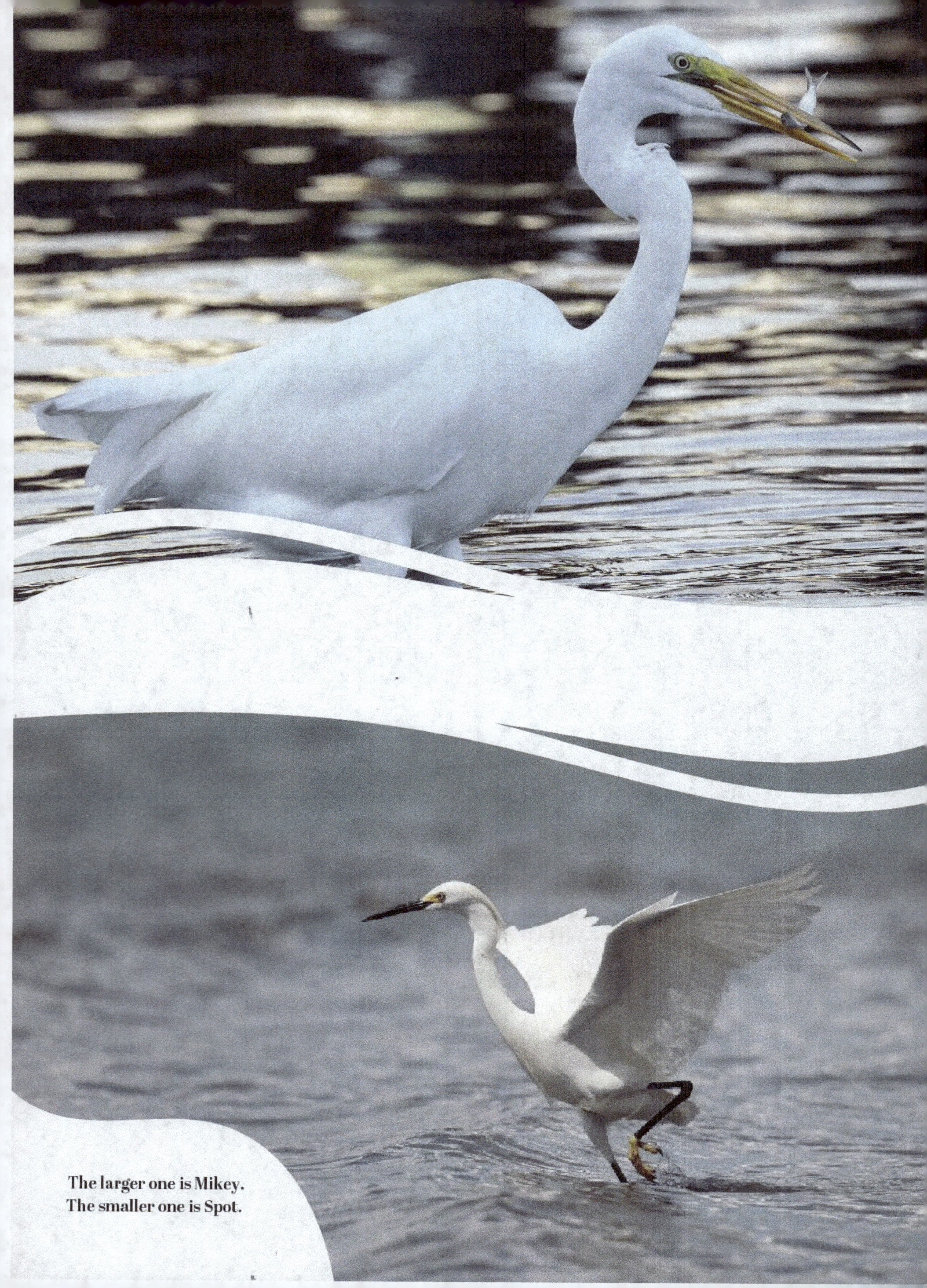

The larger one is Mikey.
The smaller one is Spot.

As the pelican glided gently through the air, eyeing the surface for a snack, he noticed a fisherman on the pier.

The fisherman was talking to a woman with a camera. Her name was Shelley. The pelican didn't know it then, but they would soon become fast friends.

One sunny day, as the pelican searched for food, he saw a delicious-looking fish floating on the surface. Without thinking twice, he dove, scooping up the fish with his gullet.

Oh no! The fish had been filleted by a fisherman and was mostly bones.

The bony fish got stuck in his gullet! It felt awful. He tried to free himself—flapping his wings, shaking his head, and even throwing his head back—but nothing worked.

The fish remained stuck. The pelican felt scared and helpless. Unable to release the carcass, he made his way to the beach where he stood shaking.

Finally, a fisherman noticed him and called to Shelley, the kindhearted photographer who knew just what to do.

"Oh, sweet bird, don't worry," She whispered. "We will help you."

She gently lifted him from the water, wrapped him in a sheet, and carried him to a floating dock nearby.

The fisherman gathered more people to help, knowing it would take several hands to help the bird. Two people held the pelican, while three others worked to pull the spiny fish from his gullet.

It wasn't easy keeping the spines from tearing his pouch. With several hands all over the pelican, he was visibly shaking with fear.

Once the fish was out, he wobbled his way back to the beach. Shelley called the bird hospital right away, but they were closed for new admissions. The person who answered told her to feed the pelican small fish he could swallow easily.

At first, he felt sick and didn't want to eat. After some rest he happily gobbled down the small fish called finger mullet. Shelley wasn't a veterinarian, but she did everything she could to help her feathered friend.

While they waited for him to get airborne again, she sat with him and kept him company. She decided to name him Pip the Pelican. She liked naming animals to help them feel like part of a family.

As the days passed, Shelley's love for Pip grew stronger and they formed an unbreakable bond.

When Pip took his first bath after his injury, Shelley let out a huge sigh of relief because this was a sign that her friend was starting to feel better.

Bathing was fun! Pip flapped his wings with all his might. They hit the water with a thud, causing the water to fly into the air.

Now that Pip was starting to feel better, he enjoyed spending time with other pelicans floating in the river, exploring, resting, and sunbathing on the sandy shore. He met turtles and other kinds of birds.

Pip and
a Cormorant

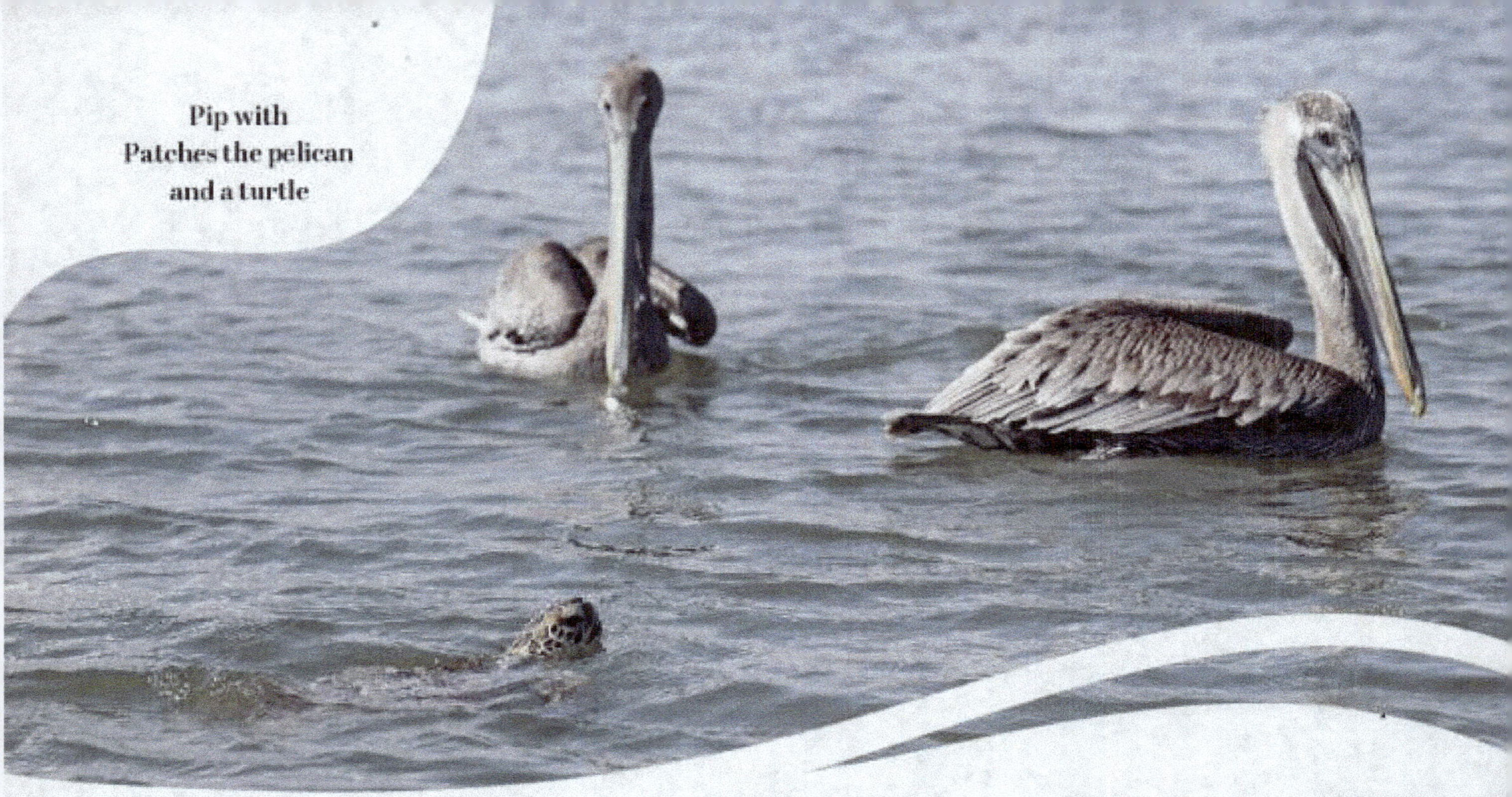

Pip with
Patches the pelican
and a turtle

Together, Shelley and Pip faced the challenges of his healing journey. She read books and sought advice from bird experts for some much-needed guidance. She watched over Pip's recovery, giving him fish and pep talks, encouraging him to regain his strength.

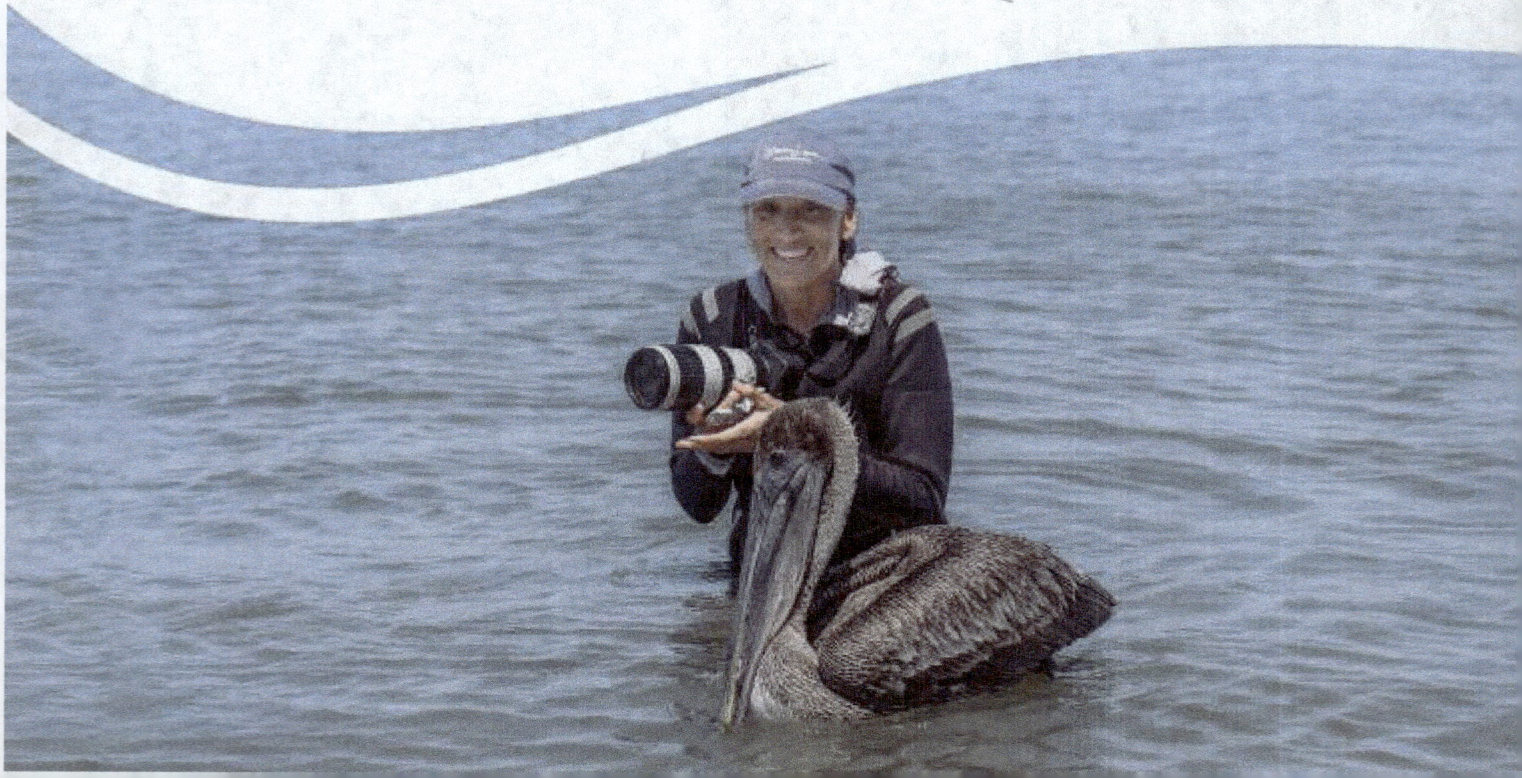

Three days after the bony fish ordeal, Pip still didn't feel well enough to fly. Being grounded can be scary for a bird.

Pip was smart and knew how to stay safe. During his time on the ground, if he wasn't under the dock, he spent time in the protective mangrove trees.

When he was hungry and Shelley wasn't around, Pip walked the docks and asked the fishermen for food.

Everyone in the community knew Pip's story and supported his recovery. Fishermen knew to give him small fish that he could easily swallow. They knew not to give him any filleted spiny fish like he'd tangled with earlier.

Walking the docks is how Pip met Mikey and Spot, the two birds he had seen earlier. They spent a lot of time together.

Mikey and Spot were good flyers and quite good at begging for fish. When they noticed the fishermen giving Pip food, they stayed close to him in hopes of getting some too!

One day, as Pip and Shelley sat on the dock, a flock of pelicans glided by overhead. Shelley said, "That's what you want to start doing, Pip. You have to fly again!" Pip looked up and Shelley could tell he was feeling a strong inner urge to fly with his feathered friends again.

The next day, Pip was finally able to fly in short bursts. His first flight after being grounded for 7 days was thrilling! Shelley squealed with excitement as he flew above the dock! She knew it meant Pip was one step closer to being healthy again.

Once able to fly, Pip returned to the same pole overlooking the lagoon to rest and heal. He liked to watch the lagoon with all the wildlife from his perch.

Once airborne, Pip still struggled to eat on his own, maybe because he was young or maybe because he was still recovering. Lucky for him, things turned around on an overcast day when he noticed a fisherman with a net standing on the dock.

The fisherman tossed a live fish to Pip! Pip's eyes widened with excitement, but those little fish were fast, and it took a couple attempts to catch one. Each successful catch brought Pip a sense of accomplishment and pride. From that moment on, he started diving and catching fish again.

Even though Pip was feeling better, he still returned to his pole each day to sleep and watch the wildlife in the lagoon.

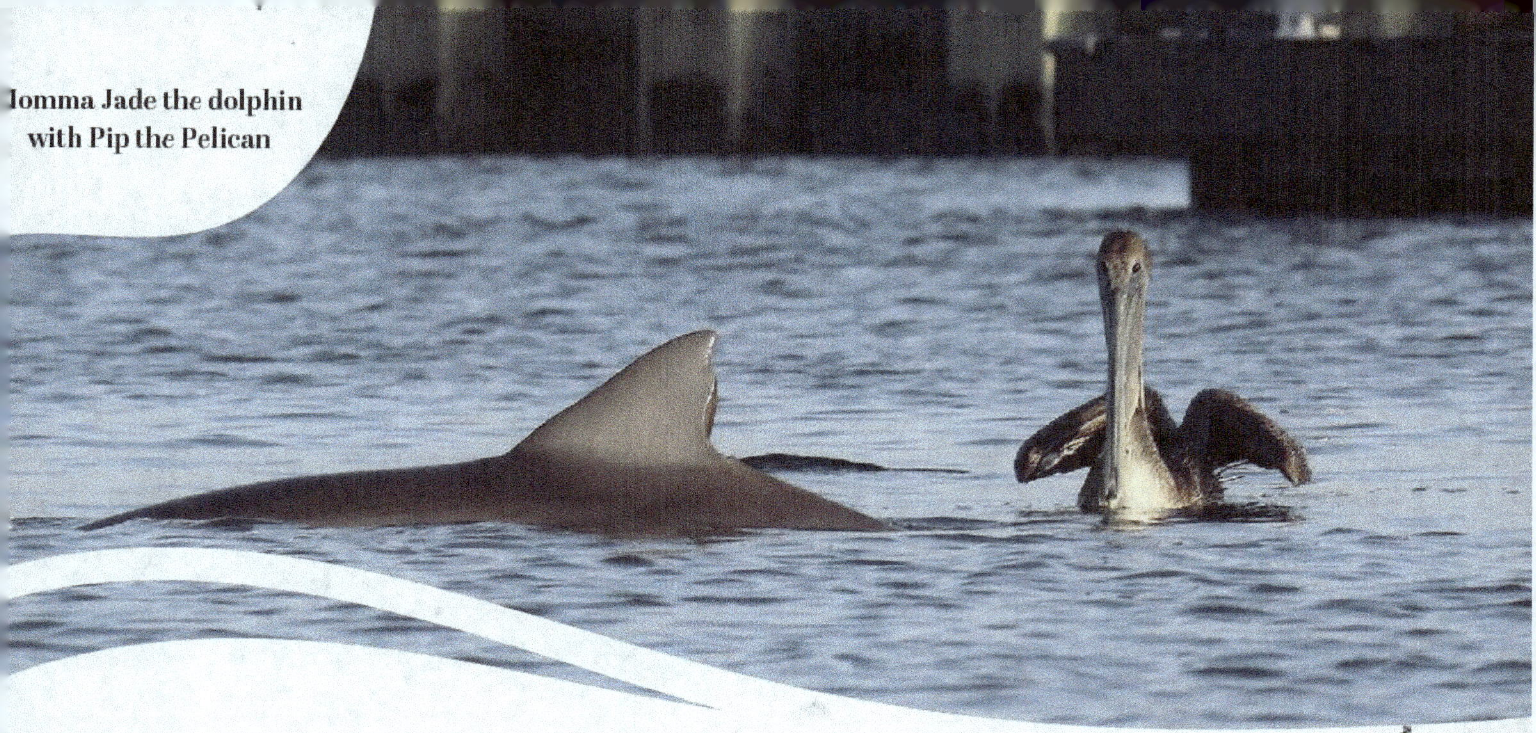

Iomma Jade the dolphin with Pip the Pelican

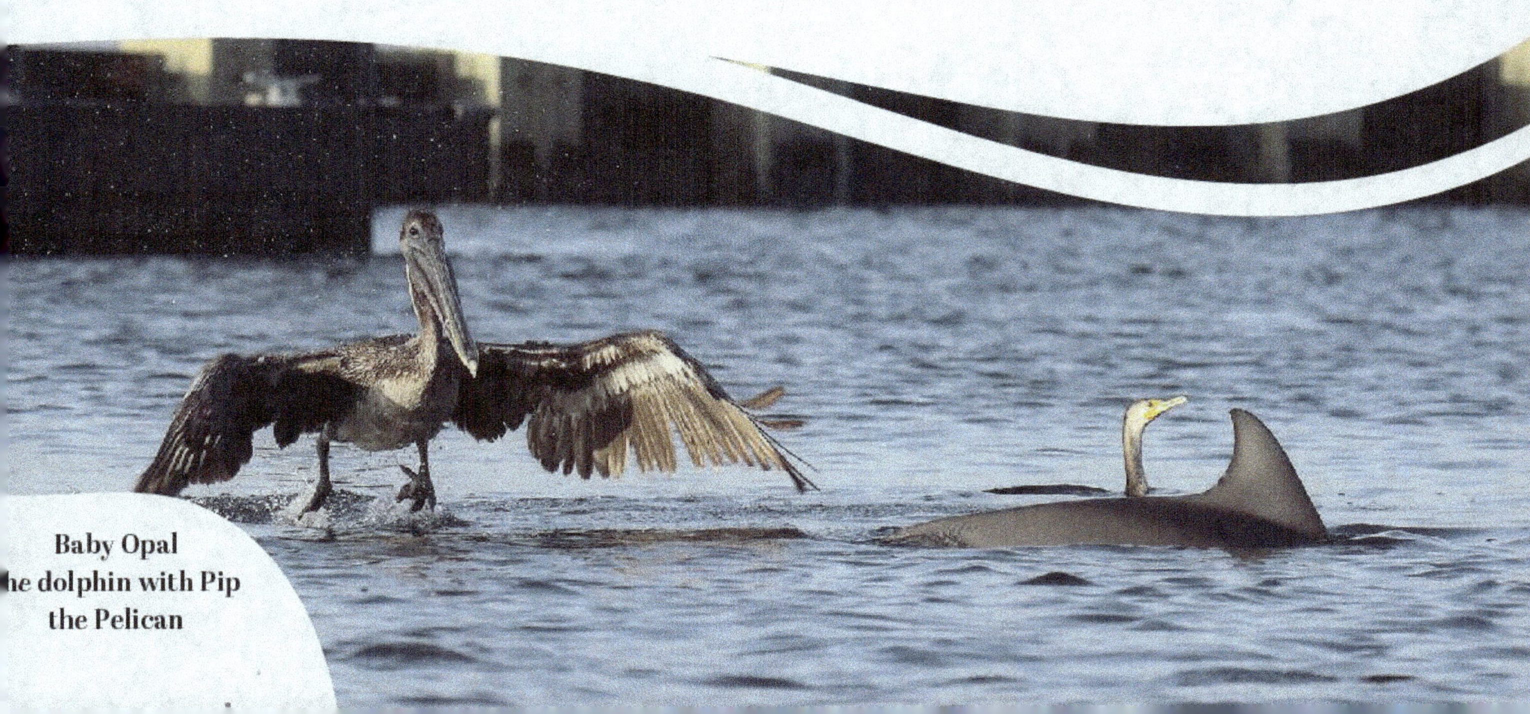

Every now and then, he would jump in the water for a fish, always avoiding the fast-swimming dolphins. However, he liked spending time with Momma Jade. She was wise and gentle, and kept him company. Pip loved her baby, Opal. Opal was nice to him. Together, they chased schools of fish and became buddies.

Baby Opal
he dolphin with Pip
the Pelican

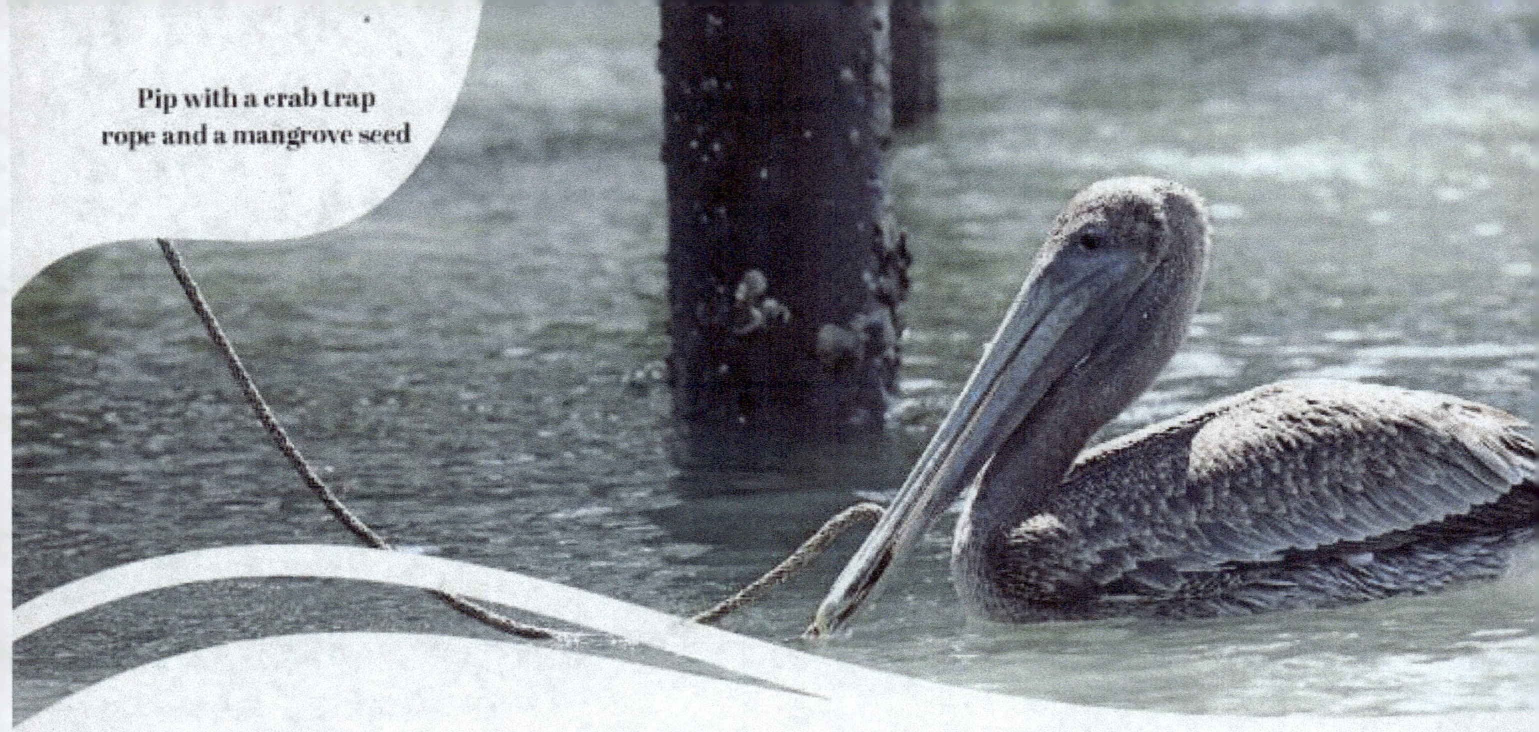

Pip with a crab trap rope and a mangrove seed

Pip found joy in simple pleasures, like tossing a stick high in the air. Soon, the mangroves became his playground rather than his hideaway. He explored the lagoon and all it had to offer.

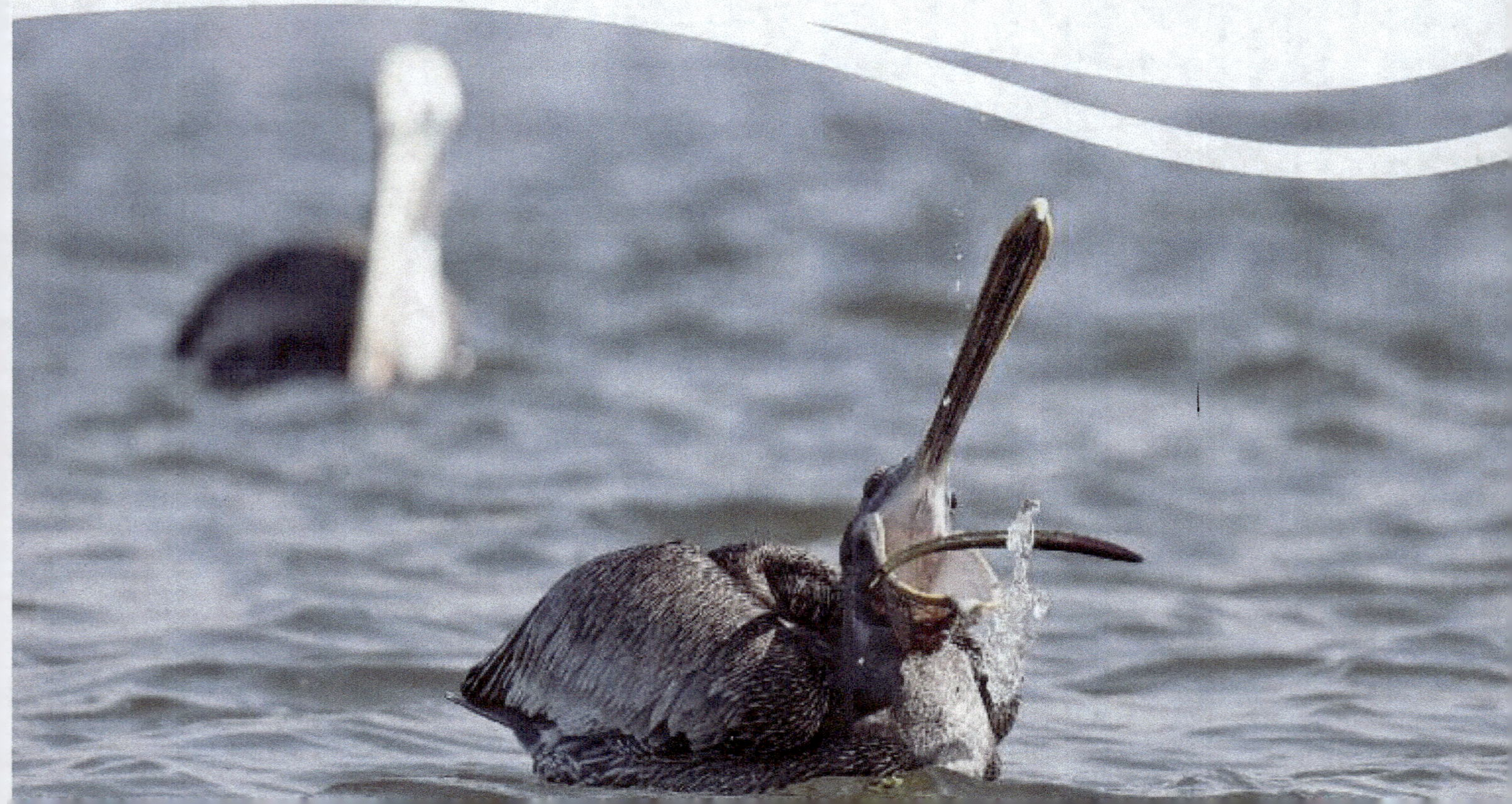

He enjoyed playing with seaweed, pulling on ropes attached to underwater crab traps and with mangrove seeds which are shaped like fat sticks.

When Shelley wasn't photographing dolphins, she and Pip took walks and played fetch. When she tossed a stick, he would chase it, toss it up with pure joy, and surprisingly bring it back to her.

Pip even learned to talk, like a bird, that is! When Shelley would ask him a question, he would exhale rapidly, making noise with his breath.

After several months of healing with the help of his lagoon family, Pip regained his strength, coming and going as he pleased. Life seemed full of promise, but little did he know that another test awaited him.

Two months after his recovery, Pip fell ill. His energy waned, and he couldn't eat. He sat on the beach, waiting for Shelley, as if he knew she would notice his condition and help him again.

Despite her efforts to help him feel better, this time, Pip needed professional help. Feeling nervous for him, Shelley drove him to a rehabilitation center in St. Augustine, Florida, seventy-five miles away.

Pip was safe in a comfortable carrier, secured for the long ride. This was his first car ride, and although it was fun to see all the horses and scenery from this perspective, he was carsick, vomiting the fish he ate. Shelley talked to him the entire ride, letting him know he was safe and explaining she was taking him for help.

Once he arrived at the rehabilitation facility, Pip was given his own room. It had a small pool filled with fish and another area with bins and bins of fish!

Truly a feast fit for a pelican. The staff said he was very weary, but with proper nutrition and medical attention, his strength would grow day by day.

After a week, Pip's health improved enough that the rehabilitation center released him. He could have stayed at the center, living just outside the fence, returning when he pleased for the endless buffet of fish. However, deep within him, a longing tugged at his heart—the call of his home, New Smyrna Beach.

Pip needed to follow his heart, so, stretching his wings and feeling determined, he bid farewell to the kind staff who cared for him, and he headed south. He took to the air, soaring with grace, strength, and confidence.

One day later, Shelley saw Pip on his pole and shouted, "Pip! You're back! I missed you, buddy."

The rehabilitation center had texted Shelley the day before to let her know he had been released. "You are amazing, Pip!" she exclaimed. "You made it back in one day!"

Apparently, the flight wasn't without struggle. Shelley noticed Pip had an injured foot.

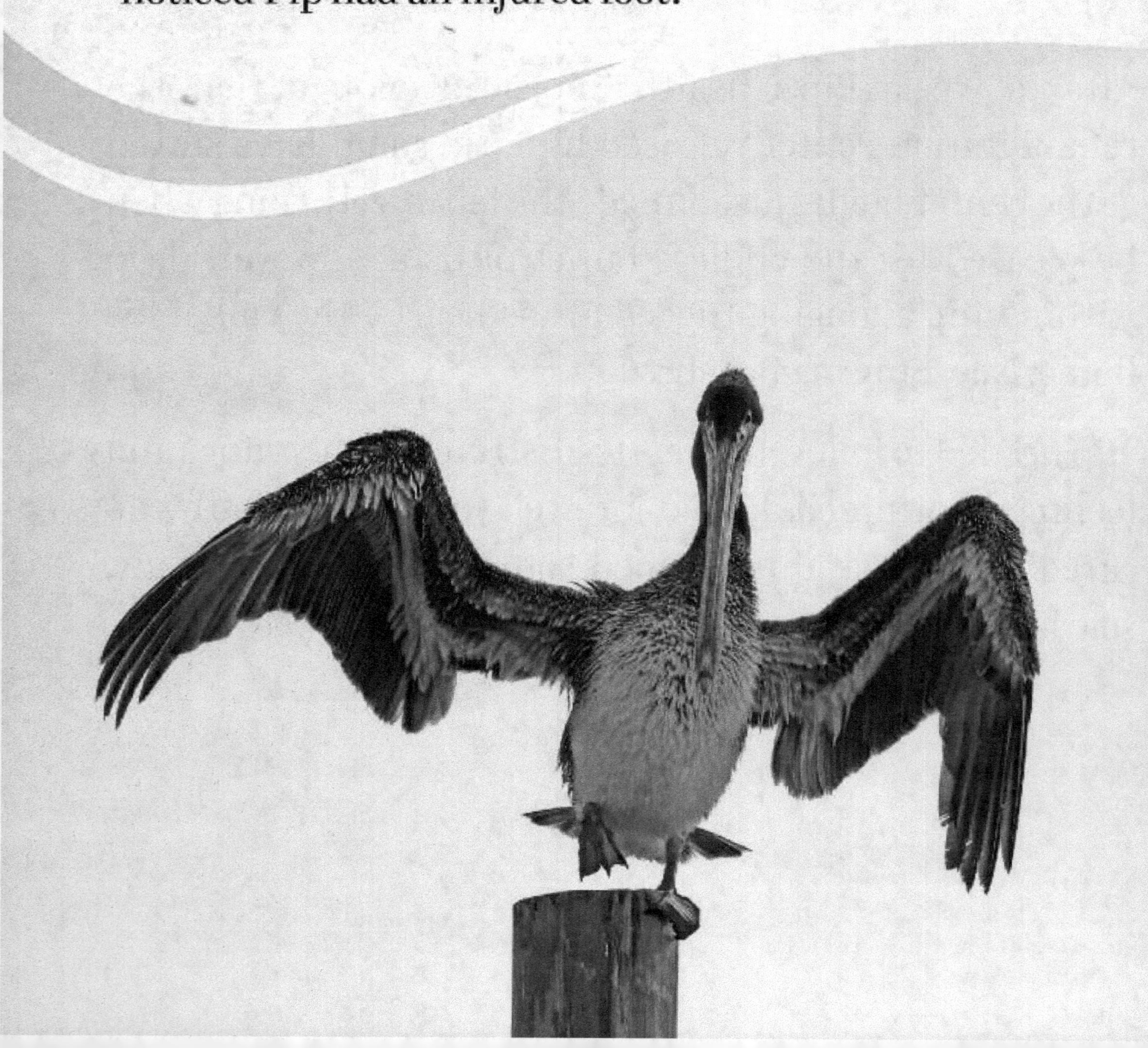

Pip knew just what to do, he rested on his pole until he felt strong again. Many people in the community stopped by to welcome him home, glad he made it back safely.

His story became a local legend, passed on from person to person inspiring all who heard his harrowing tale.

From that day forward, Pip the Pelican soared high in the sky, not only as a symbol of resilience but as a beacon of hope for all. His legacy lived on in the hearts of those who heard his tale as a reminder that home truly is where the heart is.

EPILOGUE

Pip met Shelley on March 23, 2022. They spent a year and half together visiting almost daily. However, the trauma of the sheepshead seemed to take a toll on him. He appeared to age quickly, changing his colors in a short period of time. His neck remained crooked from the bony fish making it difficult to dive for fish.

Pip visited until June 10, 2023. With a heavy heart, Shelley realized Pip had passed away. He touched the lives of many in a short time, leaving behind a legacy of love and laughter. Although he is missed, in the hearts of those who knew him, he will always soar, flying free, forever remembered, and loved.

FUN FACTS

When Shelley met Pip, his feathers were a mix of brown and white, indicating he was an immature pelican, which is just another way to say he was young. Pelicans change colors several times as they age. Just like leaves change color in the fall and winter, so do the feathers of a pelican. As they age, the old feathers fall out and are replaced by red, yellow, and dark brown feathers. Some mature pelicans have white heads, while others have yellow heads.

These 4 photos are of Pip as a mature pelican, his feathers changed from brown and white to a yellow head and eventually a white head.

Sheepshead

Sheepshead fish have dark vertical stripes running down their light gray bodies. They have sharp spines running down their backs. They also have teeth that look human.

Gullet

Pelicans have a gullet which is an extended pouch they use like a fishing net to scoop up fish.

Once they have the fish in the pouch, they tilt their head forward to drain the water then throw their head back and swallow the fish whole. It is stretchy and featherless and full of blood vessels.

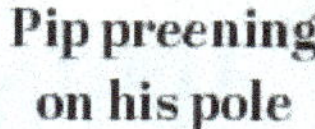

Hygiene

Pelicans take time for hygiene, too, which includes preening and bathing. During preening, they use their beaks to remove damaged feathers and bugs, as well as to spread oils around to keep the feathers in good condition for flight. This also makes room for new feathers to grow.

Mangrove Trees

Mangrove trees have many branches that twist and wrap around each other, rooting into the ground. They provide shelter for all kinds of wildlife, such as fish, crabs, and many kinds of birds. Their sturdy roots help hold the soil in place preventing erosion during storms which protects the coastline.

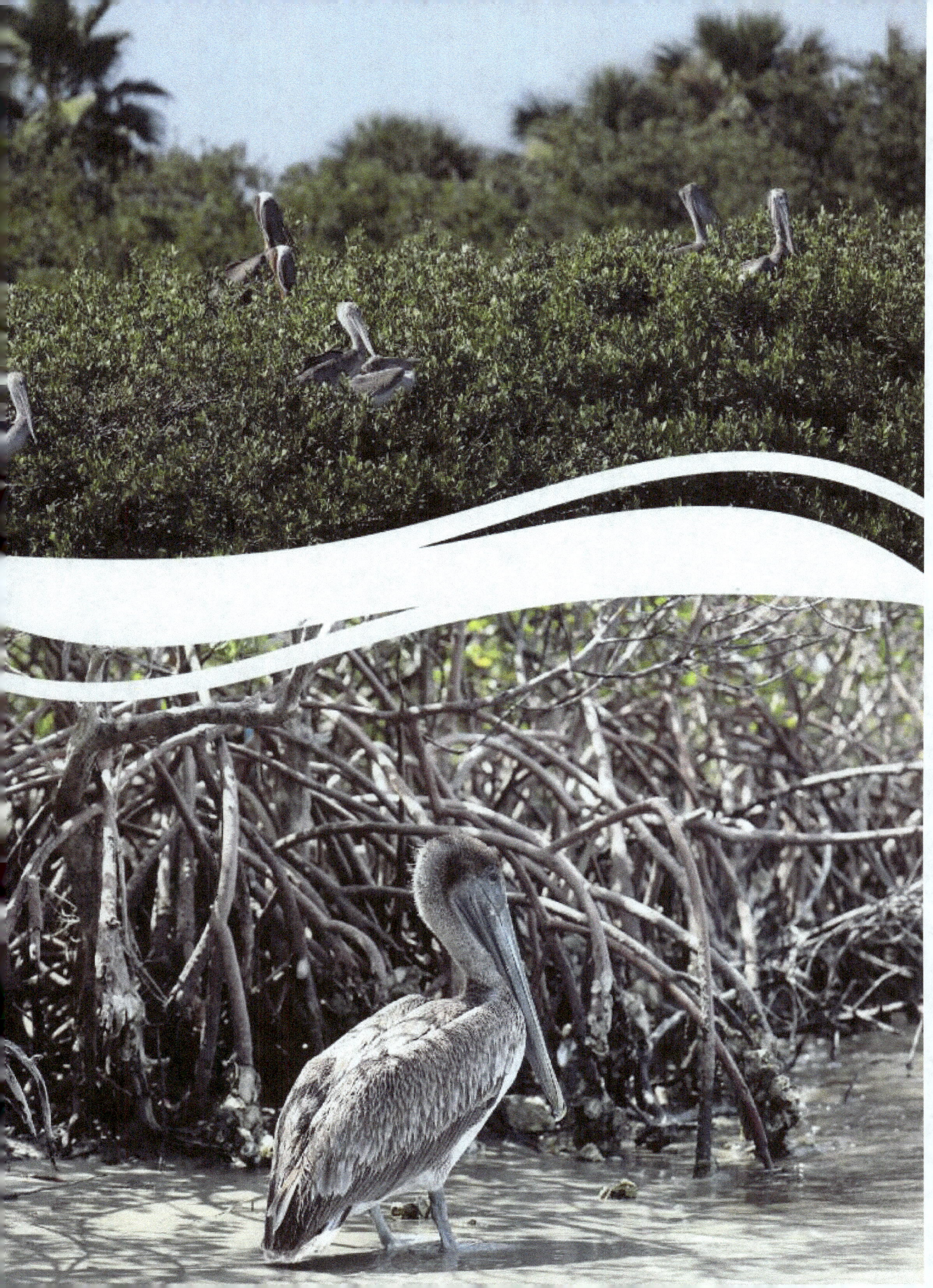

Egrets and Great Egrets

They are both members of the heron family. While egrets and Great Egrets share many physical and behavioral characteristics due to their shared family lineage, their main difference is their size.

Mikey is a great egret and is much taller than Spot who is an egret. They don't dive for fish like a pelican, they wade through shallow waters or stand on a mangrove branch and quickly grab a fish with their beak.

Egret on left,
great egret on right

Cormorants

A cormorant is a type of seabird belonging to the family Phalacrocoracidae. These birds are known for their distinctive long bodies, long necks, and hooked bills. They are skilled divers and proficient swimmers, often seen swimming in the water with just their neck and head visible. Cormorants primarily feed on fish, catching their prey underwater using their agile and streamlined bodies.

Pelicans and dolphin will often spend time together feeding. The pelicans chase the dolphins hoping to grab a fish escaping from the dolphins. Sometimes the dolphin will even toss the bird a fish!

SHELLEY AND PIP

Shelley Lynch is a multifaceted professional, blending her passion for mental health counseling with her love for wildlife photography. Since 2018, she has stood in the Indian River, capturing the beauty and grace of dolphins through her lens. As a licensed mental health counselor, Shelley brings a unique perspective to her photography, recognizing the therapeutic power of nature and wildlife in promoting well-being. Her photographs not only showcase the enchanting world beneath the waves but also serve as a testament to the interconnectedness of human and animal life. Through her work, Shelley aims to inspire others to appreciate the wonders of the natural world and to recognize the importance of preserving it for generations to come.

 **Michelle Marcus** is an educator with an unwavering commitment to nurturing young minds for over three decades. With a primary focus on lower elementary grades, Michelle has dedicated her career to instilling a love for learning in her students. Passionate and dedicated, she believes in the transformative power of education to shape bright futures. Michelle creates a supportive learning environment where every child can thrive. Michelle adds a unique educational perspective to the Pip book, ensuring that the book not only entertains but also educates.

Through their collaboration, Michelle Marcus and Shelley Lynch aspire to inspire a new generation of young readers, instilling in them a sense of wonder for the natural world and empathy for all living beings.